For Doug and Nick with oodles of love ~ J. L.

tiger tales
5 River Road, Suite 128, Wilton, CT 06897
Published in the United States 2022
Originally published in Great Britain 2022
by Little Tiger Press Ltd.
Text and illustrations copyright © 2022 Jonny Lambert
ISBN-13: 978-1-68010-269-7
ISBN-10: 1-68010-269-9
Printed in China
LTP/1400/4071/0821
2 4 6 8 10 9 7 5 3 1

www.tigertalesbooks.com

Home Is Where the Heart Is

by Jonny Lambert

tiger tales

One crisp spring morning,
Bear ambled into the
wild old woods
and decided to stay.

He built a big, bright home and
filled it with beautiful things.
But even when it was finished,
it still felt empty.

Bear
was
lonely.

So he knocked on his neighbor's door.

RAT-A-TAT-TAT!

"Hello, I'm Bear . . . ."
"Come on in!" beamed Hare.

Hare's home was very different from Bear's.
It was small, dark, and cluttered.

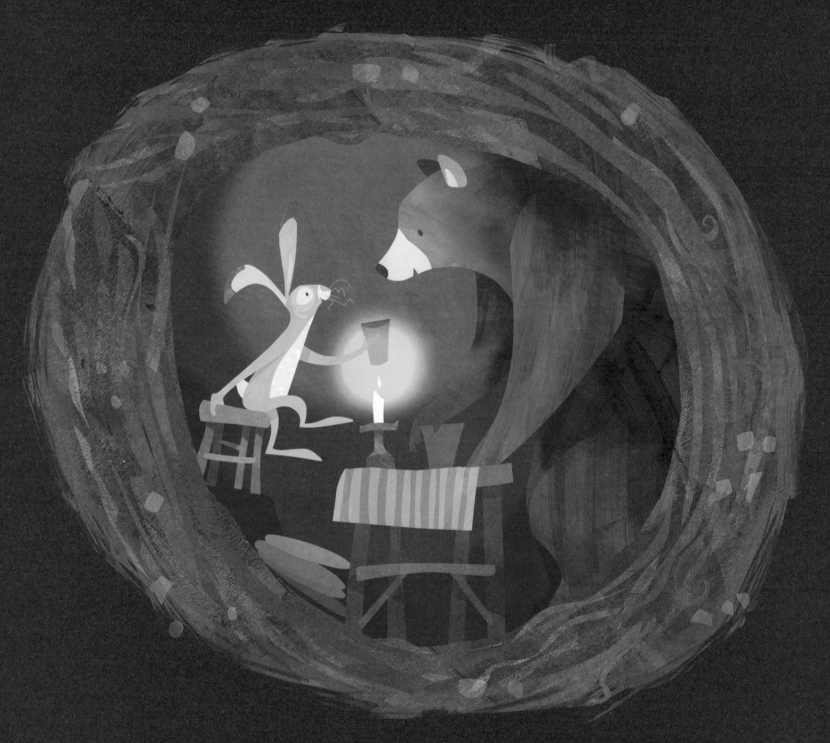

Bear and Hare were different, too.
Bear was young. Hare was old.
Hare was energetic. Bear was calm.

But they loved being together.

In spring, Hare showed Bear
the hidden wonders of the woods.
They explored every tree,
leaf, and fallen log.

In summer, they
stayed out late.
They shared delicious
picnics and played
hide-and-seek in the
warm evening sun.

When autumn turned the woods golden, Hare told Bear stories by the fire.

But as the cold set in,
Hare shivered and sniffed.
"Brrrr, Bear . . . I don't feel very well!"

So Bear cared for Hare as any friend
would, until he felt better again.

But one day in winter
came a mighty storm.
Branches snapped,
trees bent and cracked.

And in a
blinding flash
and deafening crash,
Bear's house came
tumbling down!

"M-m-my beautiful home!"
cried Bear.

He felt lost.

What would he do?

Where would he go?

Then Bear felt a gentle paw
take hold of his. Hare led
him out of the storm . . .

. . . and into the warmth.

"Come on in!"

Hare wrapped his arms
around his friend and held
him as tightly as he could.

"From now until forever,
my home is your home."

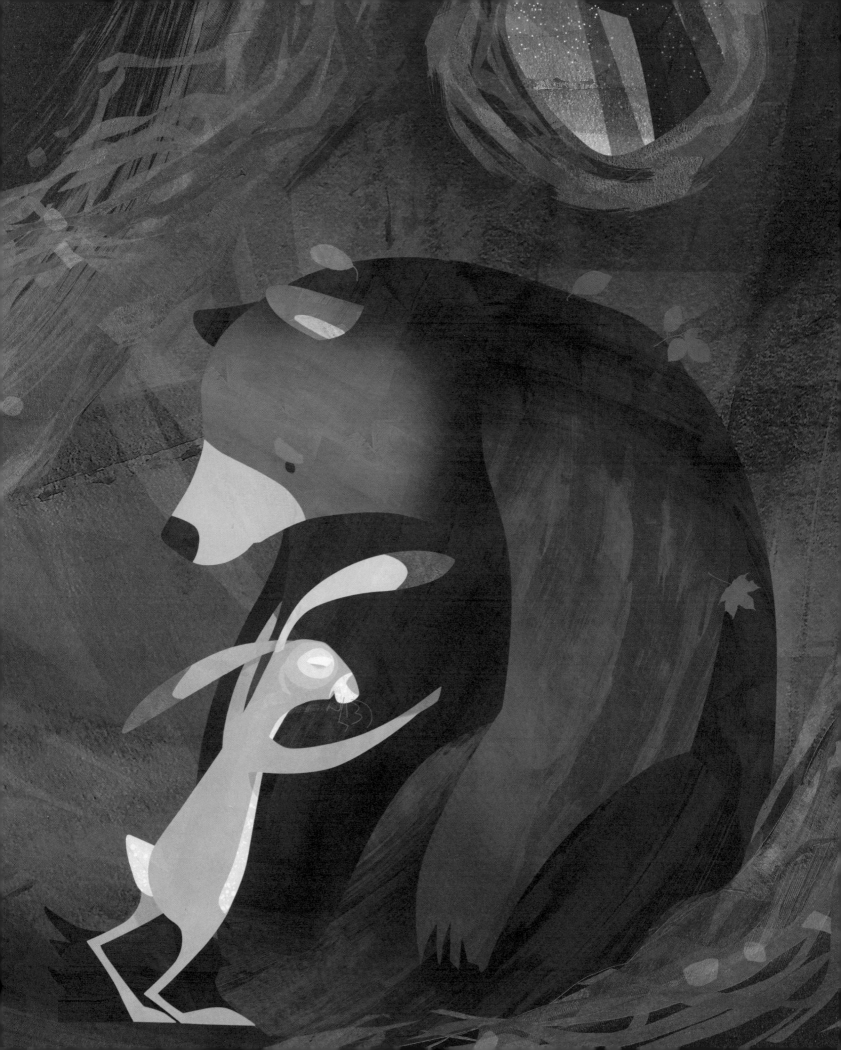

But living together wasn't always easy.

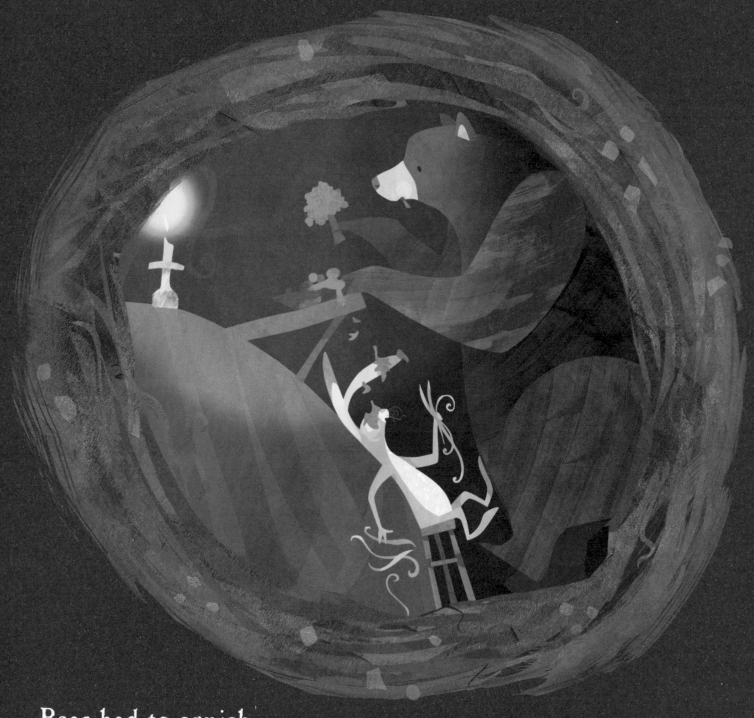

Bear had to squish.
Hare had to squeeze.

It was messy and smelly . . .

. . . all elbows and knees.

And one day, when it all got to be too much . . .

. . . they had a terrible argument!

"Hare, for the last time, STOP leaving things on the floor!"

"Don't shout at ME, Bear! Watch where you're stepping!"

Bear stormed out to sulk,
and Hare stayed in to huff.
But it was cold outside . . .

. . . and lonely inside.

Bear and Hare realized they
just couldn't live apart.

For Bear and Hare,
home simply wasn't
a place. Home was
each other.

"I'm sorry, Hare. I love you —
even though you are messy."

"I love you, too, Bear!
Even your big feet."

When spring returned to the wild old woods, there was a

RAT-A-TAT-TAT

at their door.

"Hello," said Deer.
"I've just moved here."

Bear smiled at Hare,
and Hare beamed at Bear.

"Welcome!" they replied.
"Please . . . COME ON IN!"